Little Green was proud as a pickup could be. His tires were sturdy and strong, his bumpers rubbery and thick. When his grille and front fenders were polished, he *shone*!

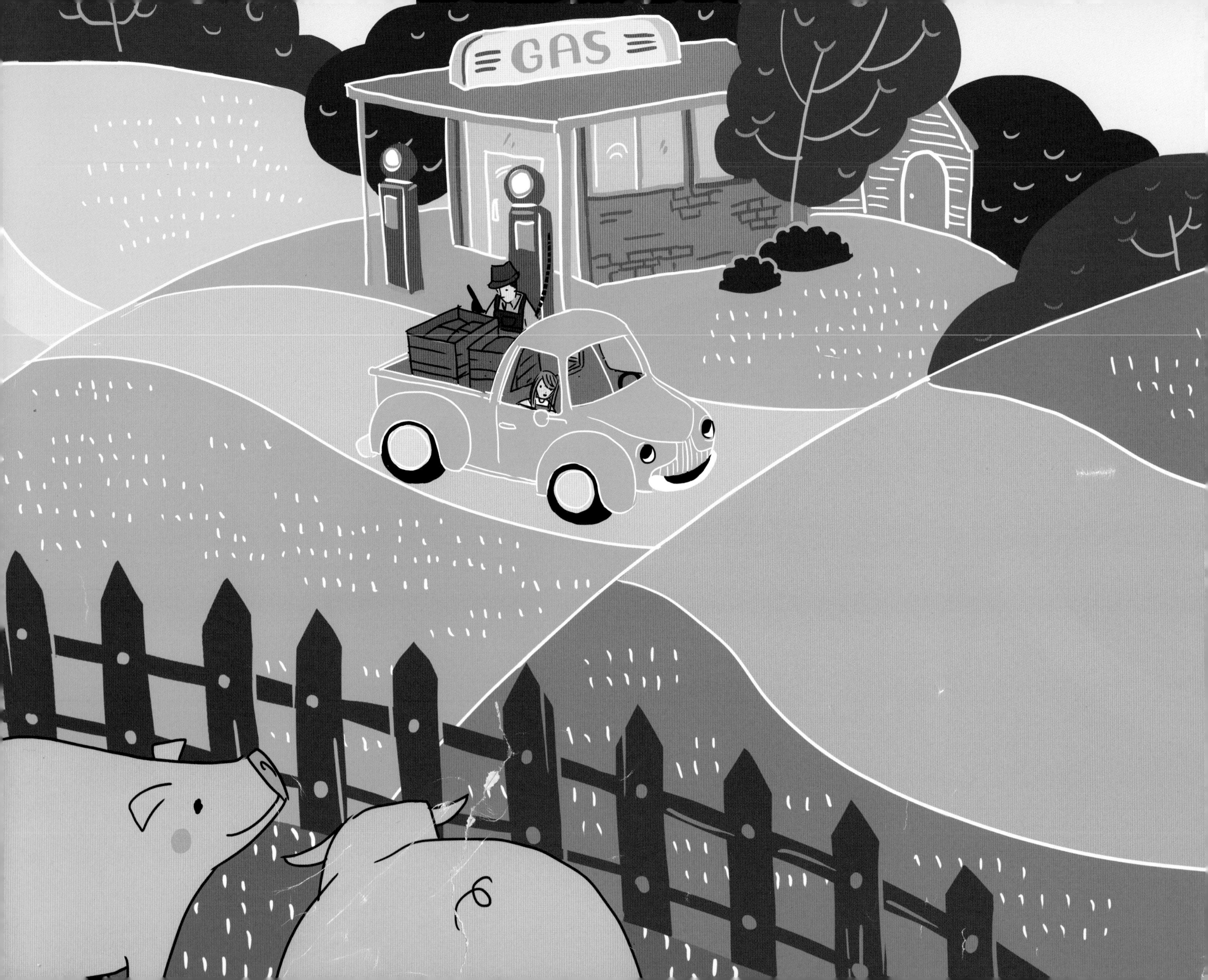
GAS

Little Green loved helping Farmer Gray and his family with chores. When Farmer Gray took him to the gas station, Little Green hummed with excitement. He liked feeling full of gas! His rear end loaded with bundles, bales, and bins—*sputter-sput-sput*—Little Green was ready. Ready to rumble down the road. He was set. Set for adventure. *Go!*

He picked up packages from the post office and groceries from the supermarket. He carted corn and soybeans to the silo and hay to the barn.

One special day, with Farmer Gray and his daughter, Fern, along to
help, he picked up two pot-bellied pigs and hauled them home to their
new sty. Little Green was a happy, busy little truck, until . . .

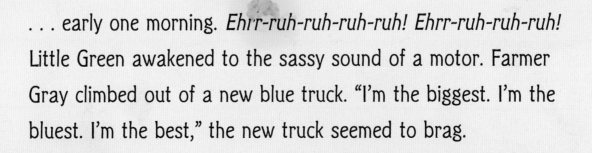

. . . early one morning. *Ehrr-ruh-ruh-ruh-ruh! Ehrr-ruh-ruh-ruh!*
Little Green awakened to the sassy sound of a motor. Farmer
Gray climbed out of a new blue truck. "I'm the biggest. I'm the
bluest. I'm the best," the new truck seemed to brag.

It was true. Big Blue had more room—more room for hay, more room for corn. She had *so* much room that she could carry *many* pigs—even goats and cows!

Farmer Gray looked happy. Farmer Gray looked proud. His farm was growing bigger and busier. Now, instead of taking Little Green to help with the chores, Farmer Gray took Big Blue. "Look how she loads," he said, patting Big Blue's side.

Now, instead of filling Little Green at the gas station, Farmer Gray left him in the meadow. Day after day, through rain and shine, Little Green sat by himself—empty and alone—with only butterflies and birds to keep him company.

Months passed. Little Green turned rusty and dirty and sad.

One spring day, after a prowl through the muddy meadow, Farmer Gray's cat jumped into Little Green's cargo bed and curled up to sun herself. Fern followed after to find her.

Missing Little Green, she too curled up in his cargo bed. Farmer Gray followed to find Fern. Farmer Gray's wife followed to find Farmer Gray. Several chickens, the pot-bellied pigs, some goats and sheep, and the family dog followed, so they wouldn't be left out.

"Papa," Fern said, "spring is here. There's a new farmers' market in town. Big Blue is too big and bumpy for city streets. Little Green is small and gentle and just right. Let's fix him up and take him."

"Great idea!" Farmer Gray said.

GR33N

So the next day, Fern and Farmer and Mrs. Gray rubbed and scrubbed Little Green until he sparkled. They changed his old rusty engine to a shiny new one. Instead of gas, they filled him with corn and soy oil from their vegetables.

Fern painted pictures of flowers, farm animals, and fruit on Little Green's sides. When Farmer Gray turned on Little Green's new engine, Little Green hummed again—a happy, hopeful tune.

Farmer Gray drove Little Green to the front of the farmhouse. He and Fern put jars of Mrs. Gray's pickled treats and crates of spring vegetables into Little Green—spinach, asparagus, and baby lettuce leaves. Now, inside *and* out, Little Green was full of vegetables!

"Look how he loads," Farmer Gray said, patting Little Green's side. "Are we ready?"

Little Green was ready! Ready for adventure. He was set. *Go!*

On the highway to the farmers' market, Little Green passed other trucks—a tow truck, a dump truck, a garbage truck, and a digger—all of them, like Little Green, busy with their chores. A few tooted their horns or blew their whistles when they passed Little Green and saw how good he looked.

At the farmers' market, everyone gathered to admire Little Green and the pictures Fern had painted on his sides. People bought Farmer Gray's fresh vegetables and Mrs. Gray's pickled ones. Children climbed on Little Green to play and munch pickles-on-a-stick. Smiling grown-ups sat to chat. Little Green was the hit of the farmers' market!

From then on, Farmer Gray used Big Blue for his big, heavy jobs, but he always used Little Green for his smaller, gentler ones . . .

In summer, Little Green carted corn and tomatoes to his new friends at the farmers' market (and—oh so carefully—the chickens' eggs and Mrs. Gray's perfect peach pies).

In fall, he carried potatoes, squash, and eggplant
(purple as autumn skies). Whatever the season,
when Little Green showed up at the farmers' market,
everyone cheered.

And Little Green?

He was happy—proud as a pickup could be!

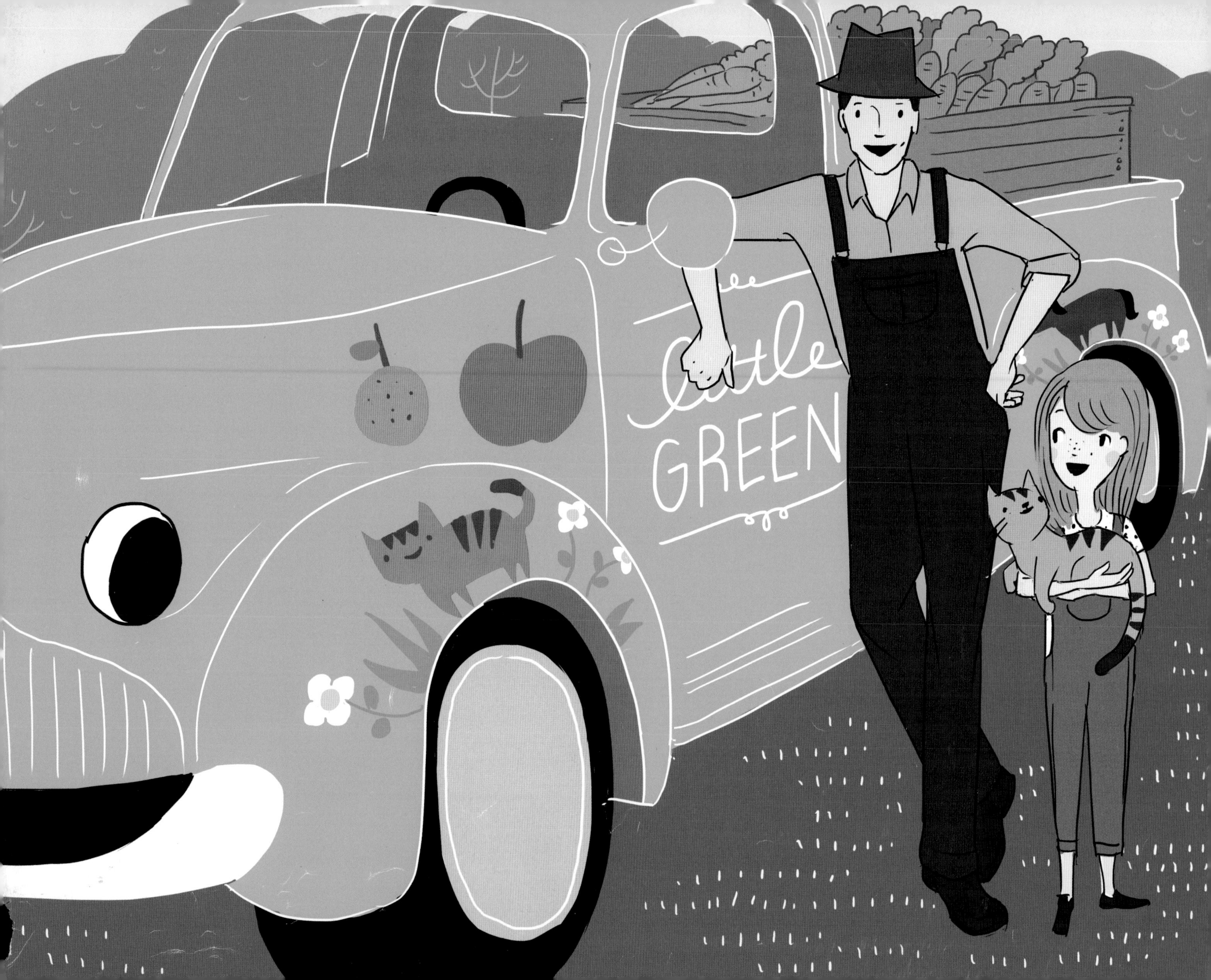
Little
GREEN

For Nathaniel Elan Goldberg and his mama, Joy Peskin,
for the inspiration.
And for Marisabina Russo
for putting us together.
—R.S.

Farrar Straus Giroux Books for Young Readers
175 Fifth Avenue, New York 10010

Text copyright © 2016 by Roni Schotter
Pictures copyright © 2016 by Julia Kuo
All rights reserved
Color separations by Embassy Graphics Ltd.
Printed in China by Toppan Leefung Printing Ltd.,
Dongguan City, Guangdong Province
Designed by Roberta Pressel
First edition, 2016
1 3 5 7 9 10 8 6 4 2

mackids.com

Library of Congress Cataloging-in-Publication Data
Schotter, Roni.
    Go, little green truck! / Roni Schotter ; pictures by Julia Kuo. — First edition.
        pages cm
    Summary: Little Green is a proud and strong pickup truck who loves helping with chores, but when
Farmer Gray buys a big new blue truck, Little Green is left to rust in a pasture until the farmer's daughter,
Fern, suggests they fix him up and use him for such gentle jobs as going to the farmers' market.
    ISBN 978-0-374-30070-8 (hardback)
    [1. Trucks—Fiction.   2. Farm life—Fiction.   3. Farmers' markets—Fiction.]   I. Kuo, Julia, illustrator.   II. Title.

PZ7.S3765Go 2016
[E]—dc23

2015003575